THE MAN
WHO COULDN'T
SEE HIMSELF

A LOVE STORY

written and illustrated
by
Richard Torregrossa

©1999 Richard Torregrossa
ISBN 1-55874-678-1

Publisher: Health Communications, Inc.
       3201 S.W. 15th Street
       Deerfield Beach, Florida 33442-8190

"Step into love for yourself,
and the universe will reflect
that love back to you."
—Melody Beattie

High up in the hills lived a man alone.

He rode the train to work every day and rode the train home every night.

He was a dry cleaner and worked long
hours making the garments of his
customers sparkle and shine.

He slept late on Sundays and got up early on Saturdays. Saturday was his busiest day.

Sometimes he had good days.

And sometimes he had bad days.

He read the newspaper in the evening
and went for walks on the weekend.

He was just like you and me in every way
except one.

He was always alone.

Alone, alone, alone. Always alone.

So he bought a dog.

The dog barked like a demon.

Especially at night. And always at the sky.
So that's what he named him—Sky.

Sky made him feel less lonely.

But only for a time. Soon they were both lonely.

So he went to a bar, but it's hard to meet someone when you're shy.

He placed an ad in the Personals section of his local newspaper. Nothing.

He even went online. But no luck there either.

He heard that yoga classes are filled with women, so he attended one, but it only made his lower lumbar region ache.

Then one day he woke at the usual hour and looked in the mirror. A very strange thing happened.

He couldn't see himself.

He was just not there.

Had he somehow disappeared, he wondered? Was he still asleep? He couldn't have disappeared because he was standing right there.

And the mirror was working because
he could see other objects in it like
his toothpaste.

And he was not still asleep because he was wide awake.

Why, then, couldn't he see himself? He must get to the bottom of this.

After he dressed, he went outside and
stood in the morning light. The sun's rays
were strong that day and everything was

bright and clear. Everything, that is,
except him. He was just not there.

Then he went to work. But everybody
could see him, same as usual.

After work he stared into a puddle to see
if he could see himself.

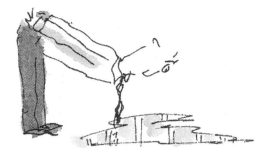

But he couldn't.

So he went to the store and bought a
new deluxe mirror. In fact, he bought a
couple.

But he still couldn't see himself. That night, frustrated by this dilemma, he couldn't sleep. It seemed that no matter what he did, he just couldn't see himself.

So he went to the doctor, but the doctor couldn't help.

Then he became depressed.

And angry.

He turned to Sky and said, "Sky, what should I do?" But Sky had no advice for him.

Finally, he just gave up. He surrendered
and accepted his fate, his loneliness.

And found his peace.

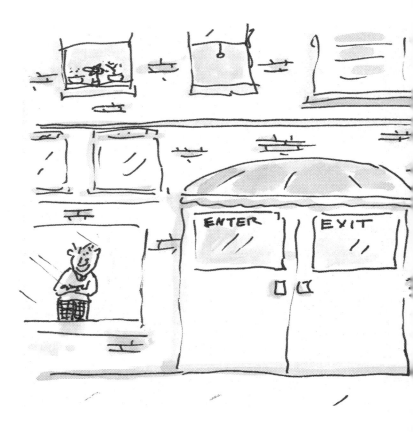

But he still had bad days.

that _YOU_ did not remove the Alaskan-Crab-sauce stain from my wife's organdy dress that you in no uncertain terms _PROMISED_ to remove! We both have access to high-powered attorneys and/or senior men on the POLICE FORCE and well-placed relatives in the MAYOR'S OFFICE. My wife needs this lovely dress for our son Jonathan's second birthday party _this evening_! She has nothing else to wear! Must she go NAKED? Or will you somehow remedy the situation?

Or should we take our business elsewhere? I hear the dry cleaner down the street is an absolute magician when it comes to removing every stain from carmelized onions to carrot vinaigrette. Well?!

But even the worst of the bad days
weren't so bad . . .

I shall, with a team of skilled professionals, take up this challenge <u>while you wait</u>. And I apologize for any inconvenience, heartache, or any other negative emotion my actions might have caused you! Please have a seat. This won't take long!

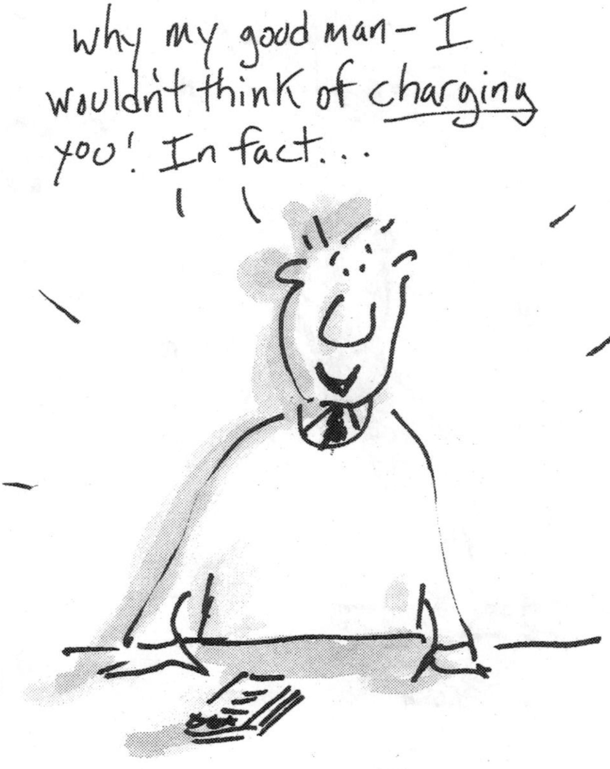
why my good man - I wouldn't think of charging you! In fact...

... make you...

They gave their paper flower to a little
girl . . .

. . . but the little girl lost it.

. . . and a man down on his luck found it.

And it made him smile.

He gave it to man's best friend, his only
friend . . .

. . . who gave it to his favorite cat . . .

. . . who gave it to another little girl . . .

. . . who gave it to a boy she liked.

He gave it to a woman . . .

. . . who was having a bad day . . .

"Thank you," she said. "A paper flower.
How sweet!"

But what I really need
is a good dry cleaner...

And she found one.

The best dry cleaner in town, in fact.

And when he saw her his heart beat so fast he thought he was having a heart attack. And he was.

But the very best kind.

"Hello," he said to her. His voice sounded big and resonant as if he was born to say the word at that precise moment.

He had a very strange feeling of destiny.
The entire world seemed to disappear.

He told her about his problem, that he couldn't see himself. But she didn't believe him, so he took her to a puddle,

then to the mirror store, and finally to the
fields of bright sunlight.

Why that's the saddest story
I've ever heard.

And her eyes filled with enormous tears.

Then it happened.

The answer! The cure! The solution! In her tearful eyes he could see himself.

And he was himself again—only better!

Then they went into a café and ordered some tea and talked and talked.

Until there was nothing more to say . . .

Then she gave him the flower that the
little boy had given her.

And never again did he have trouble
seeing himself.

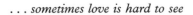

But just in case they bought him a new pair of glasses.

the
E~nd...

+he
Beginning...

Richard Torregrossa is a journalist and artist who has written for *Cosmopolitan, Self, Yoga Journal, Healthy Living,* and Microsoft's online magazine, *Sidewalk.* He also compiled and illustrated *The Little Book of Wisdom* and illustrated *Daily Meditations for Women Who Love Too Much*  by bestselling author Robin Norwood. He is the author and illustrator of five other books. *The Girl Who Has Everything* is his next book in this ongoing series of illustrated fables.

More from Chicken Soup

Bestselling author Barbara De Angelis teams up as a coauthor for this collection of stories about how people were transformed when they discovered true love. With chapters on intimacy, commitment, understanding and overcoming obstacles, couples and singles alike will look to this book as a source of love and inspiration for Valentine's Day and throughout the entire year.
Code 6463, quality softcover, $12.95

Animals bring out the goodness, humanity and optimism in people and speak directly to our souls. This joyous, inspiring and entertaining collection relates the unique bonds between animals and the people whose lives they've changed. Packed with celebrity pet-lore, this book relates the unconditional love, loyalty, courage and companionship that only animals possess.
Code 5718, quality softcover, $12.95

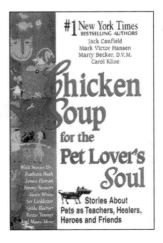